A SECOND CALDECOTT COLLECTION

A SECOND CALDECOTT COLLECTION

SING A SONG FOR SIXPENCE
THE THREE JOVIAL HUNTSMEN

Illustrated by
RANDOLPH CALDECOTT

FREDERICK WARNE

FREDERICK WARNE

Penguin Books Ltd, Harmondsworth, Middlesex, England
Viking Penguin Inc., 40 West 23rd Street, New York, New York 10010, U.S.A.
Penguin Books Australia Ltd, Ringwood, Victoria, Australia
Penguin Books Canada Limited, 2801 John Street, Markham, Ontario, Canada L3R 1B4

This edition first published 1986

This edition copyright © Frederick Warne & Co., 1986

ISBN 0 7232 3433 7

Typeset by CCC, printed and bound in Great Britain by
William Clowes Limited, Beccles and London

SING A SONG FOR SIXPENCE

R. CALDECOTT'S PICTURE BOOKS

SING a Song for Sixpence,

A pocketful of Rye;

Four-and-Twenty Blackbirds

Baked in a Pie.

When the Pie was opened,
The birds began to sing;

Was not that

a dainty Dish

To set before the King?

The King was in his Counting-house,

Counting out his Money.

The Queen was in

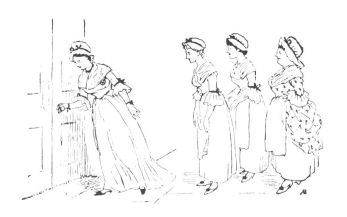

the Parlour

Eating Bread and Honey.

The Maid was in

the Garden,

Hanging out the Clothes;

There came a little Blackbird,

And snapped off her Nose.

But there came a Jenny Wren
And popped it on again.

The Three Jovial Huntsmen

R. CALDECOTT'S
PICTURE BOOKS

IT's of three jovial huntsmen, an' a hunting they
did go;
An' they hunted, an' they hollo'd, an' they blew
their horns also.

Look ye there!

An' one said, "Mind yo'r e'en, an' keep yo'r noses
   reet i' th' wind,

An' then, by scent or seet, we'll leet o' summat to
    our mind."

                           Look ye there!

They hunted, an' they hollo'd, an' the first thing
  they did find
Was a tatter't boggart, in a field, an' that they left
  behind.

Look ye there!

One said it was a boggart, an' another he said
  "Nay;
It's just a ge'man-farmer, that has gone an' lost
  his way."

Look ye there!

They hunted, an' they hollo'd, an' the next thing
    they did find
Was a gruntin', grindin' grindlestone, an' that
    they left behind.

                    Look ye there!

One said it was a grindlestone, another he said
    "Nay;
It's nought but an owd fossil cheese, that
    somebody's roll't away."

                    Look ye there!

They hunted, an' they hallo'd, an' the next thing
    they did find
Was a bull-calf in a pinfold, an' that, too, they left
    behind.

                     Look ye there!

One said it was a bull-calf, an' another he said
    "Nay;
It's just a painted jackass, that has never larnt to
    bray."

                     Look ye there!

49

They hunted, an' they hollo'd, an' the next thing
    they did find
Was a two-three children leaving school, an' these
    they left behind.

                      Look ye there!

One said that they were children, but another he
said "Nay;

They're no' but little angels, so we'll leave 'em to
    their play."

                                  Look ye there!

They hunted, an' they hollo'd, an' the next thing they did find
Was a fat pig smiling in a ditch, an' that, too, they left behind.

Look ye there!

One said it was a fat pig, but another he said "Nay;
It's just a Lunnon Alderman, whose clothes are stole away."

Look ye there!

They hunted, an' they hollo'd, an' the next thing
    they did find
Was two young lovers in a lane, an' these they
    left behind.

                  Look ye there!

One said that they were lovers, but another he
    said "Nay;
They're two poor wanderin' lunatics—come, let
    us go away."

                  Look ye there!

So they hunted, an' they hollo'd, till the setting of
    the sun;
An' they'd nought to bring away at last, when th'
    huntin'-day was done.

Look ye there!

Then one unto the other said, "This huntin'
    doesn't pay;
But we'n powler't up and down a bit, an' had a
    rattlin' day."

Look ye there!